MRS CALDICOT'S CABBAGE WAR

The Play

Vernon Coleman

This play may be performed by amateur dramatic societies without charge.

For permission to perform the play 'Mrs Caldicot's Cabbage War' please write to: publishing@mail.com giving details of your proposed date and venue, together with your name and email address.

Printed scripts are available on Amazon and since these are copyright they should not be copied without permission. The play must not be altered without consultation with the author. Please credit Vernon Coleman as the author of `Mrs Caldicot's Cabbage War' on all programmes, posters and promotional material whether printed or electronic. Thank you.

Other books about Mrs Caldicot, all written by Vernon Coleman, are: Mrs Caldicot's Knickerbocker Glory, Mrs Caldicot's Oyster Parade and Mrs Caldicot's Turkish Delight. There is also an Omnibus edition containing all four books. This is entitled `Mrs Caldicot Omnibus Edition'.

For more information about the author please visit: www.vernoncoleman.com or see his author page on Amazon.

Dedicated to Donna Antoinette Coleman, with all my love.

Cast (in order of appearance)
MRS THELMA CALDICOT (a woman in her later years)
MR GEORGE CALDICOT (Thelma's husband)
POLICEMAN
POLICEWOMAN
MR DEREK CALDICOT (Thelma's son)
MRS DORIS WARBURTON (Mrs Caldicot's Neighbour)
MR MULLER-HAWKSMOOR (nursing home manager)
MR LIVINGSTONE (nursing home resident, ex RAF)
MRS PETERBOROUGH (nursing home resident)
MISS NIGHTINGALE (nursing home resident)
HOTEL MANAGER
MS JACORANDA PETTIGREW (reporter)
MIKE TRICKLE (television chat show host)
TV CAMERAMAN (no dialogue)
STAGEHAND WITH 'CLAP' BOARD (no dialogue)
ESTATE AGENT

Sets

1. Mrs Caldicot's kitchen – a table with two chairs, cooker, fridge and work surface. There is a hat stand and a door.
2. Nursing home – split stage with lobby on the right and bedroom on the left divided by a wall. The lobby contains hooks with half a dozen coats and anoraks. The bedroom contains two pairs of bunk beds and a few bits of scruffy furniture.
3. Hotel lobby – scattered chairs and tables, with a reception desk/bar. There is a board with room keys behind the reception desk.
4. Television studio – a platform with two chairs, one or two TV cameras.

Act I Scene 1:	Mrs Caldicot's Kitchen
Act I Scene 2:	Mrs Caldicot's Kitchen
Act I Scene 3:	Mrs Caldicot's Kitchen
Act II Scene 1:	Nursing Home (lobby)
Act II Scene 2:	Nursing Home (bedroom)
Act III Scene 1:	Hotel Lobby
Act IV Scene 1:	Television Studio
Act V Scene 1:	Nursing Home

Act I Scene 1

(Mrs Caldicot's kitchen in early morning. Mrs Caldicot is making a cup of tea for her husband who is sitting at the table. He is reading a newspaper. A yellow backed Wisden is on the table in front of him. There is a pan on the stove. Mrs Caldicot pours the tea, adds milk and sugar and then stirs the tea. The spoon bangs against the side of the cup. Mrs Caldicot is wearing a pinafore and her hair has not been done. Mr Caldicot is reading a newspaper. He is wearing a crisply ironed shirt and an MCC tie. A blue blazer is on a hanger nearby, hanging on the hat stand. There is also a panama hat on the hat stand.)

MR CALDICOT: Do you have to make so much noise? Can't you stir a cup of tea without making a noise like a brass band? *(He temporarily lowers his newspaper.)*

MRS CALDICOT: I'm sorry, dear. *(She lowers her voice)* It seems to be a very noisy spoon.

MR CALDICOT: What was that?

MRS CALDICOT: Nothing dear. Just saying your toast will be ready soon.

MR CALDICOT: Is my egg ready?

MRS CALDICOT *(looking at the clock)*: It'll only be another thirty five seconds.

MR CALDICOT: Please try not to burn the toast again. It surely can't be difficult to make toast without burning it.

(MRS CALDICOT looks in the pan, lifts out an egg and puts it into an egg cup. She then puts two slices of toast onto a plate, butters it and cuts it up into soldiers. She takes the egg cup and toast to Mr Caldicot who sits waiting. He looks at the soldiers, picks one up and examines it.)

MR CALDICOT: These soldiers are too wide. *(He holds up the soldier.)* This one won't fit into my egg properly. I hate having soldiers that won't fit into my egg. *(He pushes the toast and egg to one side.)*

MRS CALDICOT: I'm sorry, dear. *(Lowers voice, speaking to herself)*. I lost my ruler.

MR CALDICOT: What was that? You seem to be mumbling a lot these days.

MRS CALDICOT: I was just apologising.

MR CALDICOT *(looking at his watch)*: Have you at least got my sandwiches ready?

MRS CALDICOT: They're in the fridge. I'll get them out. I've filled your flask.

MR CALDICOT: Ham?

MRS CALDICOT: Yes, dear. *(She takes foil wrapped sandwiches out of the fridge and puts them on the table.)*

MR CALDICOT: I can't stand cucumber. It gives me terrible indigestion. *(He stands)*.

MRS CALDICOT: I never give you cucumber, pickles, tuna, cheese, sandwich spread, tomatoes or anything with cyanide in it.

MR CALDICOT *(who has not been listening)*: I like thinly cut ham on well-buttered white bread.

MRS CALDICOT: Yes, dear.

MR CALDICOT: I can't eat brown bread. It gives me indigestion.

MRS CALDICOT: *(quietly)* Although I have heard that Tesco now make a very good arsenic and cyanide spread that tastes like French mustard.

MR CALDICOT *(picking up and holding open his briefcase)*: It's a big match today. We're playing the championship leaders. *(Mrs Caldicot puts the wrapped sandwiches and the flask into the briefcase which Mr Caldicot then closes and locks. Mr Caldicot then puts on his blazer which he takes from its hanger. The hanger falls to the floor. Mrs Caldicot picks it up since Mr Caldicot makes no attempt to do so. Mr Caldicot takes his panama hat from the hat stand and puts it on. Mr Caldicot looks down at the front of his blazer)* I've got fluff on my lapel. It needs brushing off. *(Mrs Caldicot finds a clothes brush and brushes the front of his blazer. Mr Caldicot turns round.)* Back! *(Mrs Caldicot goes round him and brushes the back of his blazer. Mr Caldicot looks down as she does so.)* Shoes need a polish. *(Mrs Caldicot goes to a cupboard, produces a shoe brush and polishes the shoes.)* Don't get the damned polish all over my socks!

MRS CALDICOT: No, dear.

MR CALDICOT: Do I look all right?

MRS CALDICOT: Aren't you putting a jumper on? It'll be windy sitting out in the open.

MR CALDICOT: The chairman of the club's sanitation committee has invited me to sit in the pavilion today. I don't want to look like a nancy boy. I've put my jumper under my shirt so that no one can see it. *(He leaves the kitchen. Wearily, Mrs Caldicot tidies up.)*

Act I: Scene 2: Mrs Caldicot's kitchen

(Mrs Caldicot is now dressed in a dowdy skirt and a dowdy cardigan. Her hair is still not done. She is mumbling to herself and scrubbing the floor. She looks exhausted. The doorbell goes. Mrs Caldicot ignores it. The bell goes again. This time Mrs Caldicot puts down her brush, holds her back and stands up. She goes to the door and opens it. A policeman and a policewoman stand there.)

POLICEMAN: Mrs Caldicot? *(He looks down at the notebook he is holding)*. Mrs Thelma Caldicot?

MRS CALDICOT: Yes? What can I do for you? If it's about the bonfire we had last Wednesday, I've got a very good explanation. It will have been the woman at no 14 who complained, won't it?

POLICEMAN: May we come in?

MRS CALDICOT *(standing aside)*: Yes, of course.

POLICEWOMAN: It isn't about the bonfire. It's rather more serious than that, I'm afraid.

MRS CALDICOT: More serious than the bonfire? Is it about Aunt Ethel? We've been expecting that. She's been dying since I was eleven. She has a weak liver and varicose veins. She's allergic to cats and takes pills.

POLICEMAN: It's not about your Aunt Ethel. I'm afraid it's about your husband. *(There is a pause, he looks at his notebook.)* Mr Caldicot.

MRS CALDICOT *(startled)*: Oh! What's wrong? Has something happened to him? I didn't put any mustard on the ham, did I? I know he doesn't like mustard.

POLICEWOMAN: I'm afraid there's been a bit of an accident.

POLICEMAN: Would you like to sit down?

MRS CALDICOT. No thank you, I'm all right standing up. I've been doing the floor. What sort of accident?

POLICEWOMAN: He was at a cricket match.

MRS CALDICOT: Yes, I know. I made his sandwiches. Ham on white bread. He won't eat cheese, pickles, tomato or tuna, you know. Well, you probably wouldn't know that, would you? Or maybe you would. You can't tell what you people know these days, can you? There aren't any secrets anymore, are there?

POLICEMAN: It was actually quite a serious accident. Are you sure you wouldn't like to sit down?

MRS CALDICOT: How can you have a serious accident at a cricket match? I've been to one. It was a long time ago but I don't think things have changed much. Nothing ever happens at a cricket match.

POLICEWOMAN: I'm afraid your husband was hit on the head by the ball they use. I'm told it's very hard.

POLICEMAN: Very hard. I had one hit me on the knee when I was at school.

POLICEWOMAN: I didn't know you played cricket at school.

POLICEMAN: I didn't. I was walking past the cricket field and this ball came out of nowhere. It still hurts when the weather's damp. *(He rubs his knee.)*

POLICEWOMAN: Mr Caldicot was apparently trying to catch it. The ball.

POLICEMAN *(looking at his notebook)*: He ran out of the pavilion, yelled 'mine' and elbowed the fielder out of the way.

POLICEWOMAN: I don't expect he felt a thing.

POLICEMAN: Except the cricket ball hitting him on the head, of course. He'd have felt that. I expect.

POLICEWOMAN: But it would have been very quick.

POLICEMAN: Oh yes. He'd have gone out like a light.

MRS CALDICOT *(who is confused)*: So what happened? Has he had to go to hospital?

POLICEMAN: He's dead.

POLICEWOMAN: He passed away immediately.

MRS CALDICOT *(disbelievingly)*: Dead?

POLICEWOMAN: One of the other spectators caught the rebound off his head.

POLICEMAN: That would have been the chair of the sanitation committee. *(He looks at his notebook.)* A Mrs Tracy Bartholomew.

MRS CALDICOT *(after a pause)*: He'd have been very proud of that. Having helped as it were.

POLICEMAN: I doubt if they would have allowed the catch. It having been taken by a spectator.

MRS CALDICOT. No, I can see that it probably wouldn't have counted. *(She pauses.)* Did you say the chair of the sanitation committee was a woman? Tracy something?

POLICEWOMAN: Yes, that would be Mrs Bartholomew. She was sitting with your husband at the time.

POLICEMAN *(reading from his notebook)*: Mrs Tracy Bartholomew, aged 46, divorcee of The Cedars, Bedlington Road.

POLICEWOMAN: She gave a statement. She was apparently very upset about Mr Caldicot's demise; said they'd been very close.

POLICEMAN: Is there anyone you'd like us to call for you? A close relative, perhaps? A father, mother, husband?

POLICEWOMAN *(quietly, to policeman)*: It's her husband who's dead.

MRS CALDICOT *(who is rather confused)*: No, no there isn't anyone to call. Oh, yes. No. Only my son Derek. You could ring him, I suppose. But he's always very busy. He's in property. *(She picks up her handbag, rummages in it, finds her diary, finds the appropriate page and hands it to the policeman who picks up the telephone and dials.)* MRS CALDICOT *(cont)*: My husband was in sewage, you know. He spent nearly all his life in sewage. He always said he was a senior sanitation engineer but I always just thought of him as being something big in sewage.

POLICEMAN: Mr Caldicot? Mr Derek Caldicot? My name is Police Constable Hobbling. I'm afraid I've got some bad news, sir. No, it's nothing to do with the tree. Yes, sir, if you say that the branch was hanging over your garden then it was your right to chop it off as long as you returned the branch to the owner. No, sir, it wasn't about that. I'm ringing about your father. Hello? Hello?' *(Turns to the policewoman.)* He's put me on hold.

POLICEWOMAN: Do you have a neighbour we could fetch while you wait for your son?

MRS CALDICOT: I suppose you could fetch the woman at no 13. She'll have seen you come to the door and she'll be desperate to know why you're here.

POLICEMAN *(now speaking on the phone again)*: Your father has been taken ill, sir. Very ill. Well, actually very, very ill. *(pause)*. Well, dead actually. Yes, dead as in not being alive. *(He pauses, listening.)* Yes, sir. *(He puts down the phone and turns to Mrs Caldicot and his colleague who have been listening.)* Your son says he's very busy but since it's a bit of an emergency he'll pop round shortly.

POLICEWOMAN: We'll go and fetch your neighbour. Did you say no 13?

MRS CALDICOT: Yes, no 13.

(The two police officers leave)

MRS CALDICOT *(to herself)*: Chair of the bloody sanitation committee. Why do they say 'chair'? Why not chairman or chairwoman? Who cares? Silly buggers. I suppose I should cry. *(She looks around the kitchen.)* I'm going to go out tomorrow and buy brown bread, pickles and a tin of tuna. I'll have a tin of tuna on a brown roll. And I'll have cheese and cucumber sandwiches. *(She picks up Mr Caldicot's Wisden which is still on the table.).* He forgot to take his bloody silly cricket book. Why would anyone keep reading the same book for a year and then buy another version of the same thing the following year? Still he won't need it now. *(She flicks through it.)* It looks about as much fun as a knitting pattern. *(She tears a few pages from it. She then stops, and looks at what she has done. But then she tears out some more pages. She doesn't stop until the book is destroyed. There are bits of the book all over the place.)* Golly. That felt good. *(She looks around.)* And I always hated his bloody chrysanthemums. Why couldn't he grow roses or delphiniums occasionally just for a change? Always chrysanths for 30 years. I never liked them. They're like politicians: all show and no substance. I bet SHE liked them. The chair of the sanitation committee. Bloody missus whatever her name is. *(She picks some chrysanthemums out of a vase, cuts them very short and puts the heads into a tea cup.)* There. That's better. Cut you down to size, haven't I? What else is there? *(She opens a door and brings out a bag of golf clubs. She then finds a large saw and smiles.)*

Act I Scene 3

(Mrs Caldicot's kitchen. There are sawn off bits of golf club everywhere. Mrs Caldicot looks dishevelled but pleased with herself. There are also bits of Wisden and flower stalks on the table and the floor. The doorbell goes. Mrs Caldicot answers it and her son stands there.)

MRS CALDICOT: Oh, hullo, Derek. *(She sounds rather surprised to see him. She does not seem excited or pleased by his presence.)*

MR DEREK CALDICOT: I was so sad to get the news. Hit on the head with a cricket ball, eh? What a way to go? He went quickly I expect. And he loved cricket so it would have been a good end for him.

MRS CALDICOT: His fancy woman caught the ball after it bounced off his head.

MR DEREK CALDICOT *(startled)*: His fancy woman? What…? *(He suddenly notices the bits of golf club and so on strewn about)*. Mum! What's happened?

MRS CALDICOT *(also looking around, as though surprised by what she sees)*: Oh. I haven't had time to tidy up.

MR DEREK CALDICOT *(picking up a piece of a golf club)*: This was a very nice special graphite shafted pitching wedge with parabolic cross hatch grooves. I could have used this. *(He stoops and plays an imaginary shot with half a club.)*

MRS CALDICOT: I think your father dropped his bag and they all broke.

MR DEREK CALDICOT: *(picking up pages of the Wisden)* And his Wisden! I suppose he dropped this too? My father would die if he saw this.

MRS CALDICOT: No, he wouldn't. *(Derek looks at her.)* He's already dead.

MR DEREK CALDICOT *(taking one of the flowers from the tea cup)*: And what happened to his chrysanthemums?

MRS CALDICOT: They're a new dwarf variety.

(The doorbell goes. The neighbour arrives. She enters oozing sympathy.)

MRS WARBURTON: I'm from number 13. Oh, my dear, how awful. What a shock you've had. You poor thing. *(She puts her arm around Mrs Caldicot and pats her on the back.)* The police told me all about it. They said you'd asked for me specially.

MRS CALDICOT *(to Derek)*: This is my neighbour from number 13. Mrs ...er… *(she clearly does not know the neighbour's name).*

MRS WARBURTON: I'm Doris. Doris Warburton. *(she addresses Derek).* I'm next door but five. It's the only house with the glassed in porch.

MR DEREK CALDICOT: I'm Mr Caldicot. *(Neighbour looks puzzled.)* The son.

MRS WARBURTON: Oh yes, of course. *(she laughs lightly).* Silly me. I was confused for a minute then. What a shock it's been for you both. I know what it's like to lose a loved one. When my Bert died I was in shock for months. The doctor gave me three different tranquillisers and two different types of sleeping tablet. That was fourteen years ago. I'm still on them, of course. He was a wonderful man. He did a lot of fretwork and kept budgerigars. My husband, not the doctor, though he might have done I suppose. I had to get rid of the birds when he passed on. But I kept the fretwork. *(For the first time she notices the bits of golf club and so on.)* Oh dear. Has there been an accident? I didn't know they were fragile like that.

MRS CALDICOT: The golf bag fell over and the clubs broke. You wouldn't think they'd be so fragile, would you? They don't make things like they used to, do they? They were probably made in China. The flowers are a new dwarf variety. And that cricket book sort of came apart. A problem with the binding, I think.

MRS WARBURTON: Ah!

MR DEREK CALDICOT *(to his mother)*: I ought to ring the doctor. Fix up some pills for you. And we'll have to think about the future, mother. You won't want to stay here by yourself, of course. We'll have to think about finding you some sheltered accommodation. My firm owns a nice nursing home not far from here. I've got a bit of clout with the management and I'll see what I can do about getting you in straight away. *(He looks around).* Then we can set about selling this old place and releasing some of the equity. You don't want your money all tied up in bricks and mortar at this time of your life do you, mother?

MRS CALDICOT: A nursing home? Why do I need to go into a nursing home? I'm not that old! I'm not falling apart yet!

MR DEREK CALDICOT: Well, you obviously can't stay here by yourself, can you? You'll need looking after. What about if there's an emergency? A fall or something?

MRS CALDICOT: I've been looking after myself quite well, thank you. And I was looking after your father too. *(Pauses)*. He took a lot of looking after.

MR DEREK CALDICOT: Don't be difficult, mother. You leave everything to me. *(He takes out a mobile phone.)* What's the doctor's number?

MRS CALDICOT: I don't know. I haven't seen a doctor for years. *(She picks up her handbag.)* I'll have to look it up. *(She takes out an old-fashioned diary, finds the relevant page and hands it to her son, pointing out the relevant page on the address book at the back. Derek dials the number she shows him and walks away to another part of the kitchen while he telephones the doctor.)*

MRS WARBURTON: You sit yourself down, dear, and I'll make you a nice cup of tea. *(She looks around, spots the kettle, and sets about making a cup of tea. There is lot of clattering and banging as she does so. Derek looks daggers at her as he struggles to make the phone call.)* Have you got any brandy? I've read that brandy is good at a time like this.

MRS CALDICOT: There's a bottle of cooking sherry in the cupboard. Mr Caldicot keeps it for his indigestion.

MRS WARBURTON: Oh, my Bert was a martyr to indigestion. Don't get me on that. I could talk for hours about his indigestion. He was ruled by his stomach. Couldn't eat anything that was green, orange or yellow and he wasn't too good with anything brown. It didn't leave a lot. *(She finds the bottle of sherry and brings it out.)* Shall I pour you one too, dear? *(She pours herself a generous sherry and knocks it back.)*

MRS CALDICOT: No thank you. I hate the stuff.

MRS WARBURTON *(She waves the bottle in Derek's direction. He looks hard at the bottle, shudders and shakes his head.)*: Well, I'll just help myself to another if you don't mind. I've read that it's good for combating shock and stress. *(She has a second generous sherry)*.

MR DEREK CALDICOT *(switching off his phone and putting it away)*: The receptionist said the doctor is terribly busy and can't come. But she says she'll get him to sign a prescription for some tranquillisers. I'll pop down and get them. The receptionist says you'll need them straight away and they've got a pharmacy at the surgery. I'll call in at the undertakers too and get them booked. Cremation, two hymns and five minutes from the vicar all right? There's no need for a feast afterwards, is there? Don't think so. Bit of a waste of money. I'll pop down to the doctor's. *(He leaves.)*

MRS WARBURTON: You can have one of my pills, love, while you're waiting. I've got plenty. My doctor gives me 200 at a time whenever I ring up. I haven't seen him for years, he's always too busy signing prescriptions I expect, but he's very good with letting me have more pills. *(She rummages in her handbag.)* I always carry them with me for emergencies. *(She takes a bottle of pills out of her handbag, shakes out a capsule and hands it to Mrs Caldicot. Then she changes her mind and shakes out a second.)* I think I'll have one too. Good for shock. *(She pops one into her mouth and takes it with a swig of sherry straight from the bottle. She then pours Mrs Caldicot half a glass of sherry.)* Here you are, dear. You'll need this. You can't swallow pills without something to wash them down with – especially not tranquillisers. *(Mrs Caldicot takes the capsule and the sherry and swallows both.)* There you are dear, that'll put a lining on your stomach. *(She laughs and pours another sherry.)* Now have another drinky to wash it down properly.

MRS CALDICOT *(swallowing)*: Thank you very much. *(She coughs.)*

MRS WARBURTON: Oh dear. That's gone down the wrong way. Wasted now. You'd better have another. *(She hands Mrs Caldicot another capsule and another sherry.)* I'd better have one too otherwise you'll be drinking on your own and they always say that's the slippery slope to somewhere. *(The two women drink silently.)* Doctors are wonderful these days, aren't they? In the old days they wouldn't give you pills unless you rang up, made an appointment, sat there, waited and then answered a lot of rude questions about your bowels and other habits. Sometimes they even made you get undressed. *(Pauses, sips her sherry and remembers.)*

When I was younger the doctors always used to want to listen to my chest. *(Pauses and sips again.)* No one's listened to my chest for years. *(she sighs.)* Still, these days it's all much easier. You ring up, speak to a receptionist and then pop down and pick up a nice, big bagful of pills. Wonderful. It's progress I suppose. Have you finished that yet?'

MRS CALDICOT: What? Oh my drink? *(She looks at her glass which is still half full)*. No, not yet, thank you.

MRS WARBURTON: Well, you'd better have a drop more anyway. I know I will. *(She pours them both more sherry.)* You know I'm not entirely sure there are any doctors these days. You never see them do you? In the old days, before progress took over, you could ring them up, any time of day or night, and they'd pop round with their little, black bag and sort you out. They were there at the other end of the phone. These days they work the same hours as the council and you'd stand as much chance of getting the dentist or the public librarian to visit you at home as of getting the doctor to come out. My friend, Mrs Bunting, she lives in Templeton Avenue, between the new mosque and the other one, the what's it called, the synagogue, she was in hospital for a week and she only saw a doctor once. Even then she says she wasn't sure he actually was a doctor. Not a real doctor. He had a white coat but then everyone in hospital has a white coat these days don't they? She said she did think he might have been a porter because he didn't speak any English but that doesn't mean anything does it? She said she thought she did see a nurse on the Wednesday but that was about it. Still, we mustn't grumble. It's much easier to get the pills these days so that's a big improvement, isn't it?

MR DEREK CALDICOT *(Who has returned and is slightly out of breath with a bag of pills in his hand)*: There you are mother, a nice bag of pills. The blue ones are to relax you, the red ones are to help you sleep and the green ones are for something else – possibly to wake you up. There are 100 of each to start you off with but the receptionist says you can get more whenever you like now that they've put you on their computer. You're to take two blue ones every four hours, two red ones at night and the green ones whenever you feel like it. I've booked the crematorium for Thursday at 12.17 and got you a good price because they had a cancellation. I've arranged for a nice economy casket with handles they can unscrew and use again. You get a free cardboard urn for the ashes. Best of all I've fixed up for you to move into the Twilight Years Nursing Home on Thursday after the crematorium. It'll help make sure you don't spend too much time grieving. You'll meet lots of new chums, lots to keep you busy. They do sitting down keep fit on alternate Wednesdays and bingo on alternate Saturdays throughout the winter except December so you won't have time to be bored. I'll arrange for the auctioneers and estate agents to come in on Friday to clear out the furniture and put the house on the market. *(He kisses Mrs Caldicot on the head.)* Must dash now I've got a meeting with JB in Wolverhampton twenty minutes ago. *(He rushes out.)*

MRS WARBURTON: Wonderful young man. Is he always in a rush?

MRS CALDICOT: He was two weeks premature.

MRS WARBURTON *(She opens up the bag of pills and examines them.)*: Oh, I've not seen these green ones before. Let's try a couple. *(She fetches the sherry and two glasses. She looks at the bottle which is almost empty.)* Have you got any more of this? It tastes better the more you drink of it.

Act II: Scene 1

(The Nursing Home. The set is divided into two. On the left there is the bedroom and on the right there is the lobby. This scene is set in the lobby.)

MR MULLER-HAWKSMOOR: Come in, come in! Welcome! Welcome!

MR DEREK CALDICOT: This is my mother, Mrs Caldicot. Mother, this is Mr Muller-Hawksmoor, the executive manager of the Twilight Years Rest Home.

MRS CALDICOT *(very sleepily)*: How do you do?

MR MULLER-HAWKSMOOR: Marvellous to see you. Wonderful. Terrific. What a pleasure! *(suddenly puts on a sympathetic face and voice)*. So, so sorry to hear of your sad loss, of course. Very sad. Very sad indeed. *(resumes jollier mode)*. But we'll make you happy here. Soon help you forget. You'll fit in very well. Lots of friends around. Always something going on. Sitting down keep fit classes on alternate Wednesdays in May, when our teacher is available and bingo on alternate Saturdays throughout the winter months except November, December, January and February. You'll be rushed off your feet. Did you bring your tablets with you?

MR DEREK CALDICOT *(handing over a bag of pills)*: I've got them!

MRS CALDICOT *(sniffing)*: What's that awful smell?

MR MULLER-HAWKSMOOR: Oh, that will be luncheon. Chef was running a little late today and we find that in any case the aroma of good cooking always lingers a little longer. Our chef used to work at a popular restaurant on the M6 and would have Michelin stars if the judges were a little less snooty. We always get the very best ingredients and sometimes that means meals get delayed a little.

MR DEREK CALDICOT: It's a very nice smell!

MRS CALDICOT: It smells like cabbage. *(turns to Derek)* You never ate cabbage when you lived at home. You always said the smell of it made you feel sick.

MR DEREK CALDICOT *(trying to smile)*: Oh no, not at all. Cabbage was always my favourite vegetable.

MR MULLER-HAWKSMOOR: Oh yes, there will be cabbage and I make no apology for that. Cabbage is a wonderful, undervalued vegetable. Too often derided. Scorned even. But full to the last leaf with vitamins and minerals which are essential for healthy living. We take nutrition very seriously here. None of our residents goes short of vitamins and minerals. Not if we have anything to do with it. Our consultant dietician, whose book we refer to often, insists that cabbage is an integral part of the daily diet.

MR DEREK CALDICOT *(looking at his watch)*: Is it possible for my mother to see her room? I've got a property foreclosure to see to in 30 minutes and then I've got a meeting with the agent who is handling the sale of mother's house and the auctioneer who is getting rid of all the furniture for us. (Mrs Caldicot looks puzzled and confused.)

MR MULLER-HAWKSMOOR: Of course. Straight away. You'll be very comfortable here, Mrs Er…Caldy. A home from home as we say. *(He leads the way through a connecting door into a bedroom. There are two pairs of bunk beds in the room. Three bunk beds are occupied with patients who appear to be asleep.)* Here we are. One of our premier rooms – the Windsor Suite. We like to keep everything compact so that our residents have everything they need close at hand. All our furniture and bed linen items are made from natural man-made plastics and fibres which offer cleanliness, style and a feeling of old-fashioned solidity. *(Mrs Caldicot touches a table which collapses.)*

MR DEREK CALDICOT *(cheerily)*: No risk of getting lost in here!

MR MULLER-HAWKSMOOR: Certainly not. But all mod cons are provided. There's a bathroom just down the hall with night time facilities provided en suite at no additional cost. *(He pulls two chamberpots from underneath the two lower bunks, looks into them, pulls a face and quickly pushes them back.)* Those are usually emptied regularly on a daily basis. I will have a word with matron later.

MR LIVINGSTONE *(who is on one of the top bunks, wakes up and looks down)*: What's going on?

MR MULLER-HAWKSMOOR: Ah, Mr Stanley! Having a little nap are we? *(He turns to Derek)*. We encourage our guests to take a siesta after luncheon. The older mind and body needs extra rest and our consultant physician, who telephones me every three months whether it is required or not, is a firm believer in providing guests with all the medication they require to take the necessary hours of rest. She is a much loved and qualified general practitioner who works for an internet provider of health care and she doesn't see the individual guests, of course, but she renews her instructions for medication when we speak on the telephone. We don't like to encourage our guests to think of themselves as patients so we prefer it that she doesn't actually see them.

MR DEREK CALDICOT: That's splendid! *(He turns to Mrs Caldicot.)* Isn't it mother? *(Mrs Caldicot stares at him but doesn't speak.)*

MR LIVINGSTONE *(climbing down from his bunk bed)*: Are those really vitamin pills the nurses give us after lunch? They always make me feel very sleepy. And my name is Livingstone, by the way, not Stanley. *(The two women in the lower bunks now awake and look around sleepily before climbing out. These are Miss Nightingale and Mrs Peterborough.)*

MR MULLER-HAWKSMOOR: And here are your other two roommates, Miss Er and Mrs Um.

MRS CALDICOT: Do I have to share a room?

MR MULLER-HAWKSMOOR: My word yes. Oh yes. We like to encourage our valued guests to think of this as their home and an eminent consultant psychologist, whose book I regard as a useful source of information, has said that sharing a room with other guests helps to cement that feeling of companionship and to create real and lasting bonds and a sense of 'home'. *(He locks the fingers of both hands to illustrate what he means.)* Once you're here, Mrs Er…, you will simply be exchanging the bosom of one wonderful, loving family for the bosom of another.

MRS CALDICOT *(looking at Derek)*: That's reassuring.

MISS NIGHTINGALE: Have you come to empty the bed pans? They haven't been done since last Tuesday.

MR MULLER-HAWKSMOOR: One of our trained nursing aides will be along shortly to deal with that.

MISS NIGHTINGALE: I hope she isn't going to be too long. *(Hops from one foot to the other)*. They're full.

MR MULLER-HAWKSMOOR *(to Derek and Mrs Caldicot)*: Some of our guests are a little self-centred and fail to see the bigger picture. *(He turns to Miss Nightingale.)* You could use the facilities in the first floor bathroom.

MR LIVINGSTONE: It doesn't work. There's a blockage. It seems to be full of cabbage.

MR MULLER-HAWKSMOOR *(furious)*: One of our nursing aides and our fully trained visiting plumbing specialist will deal with all these little problems in due course. *(Turns to Derek and Mrs Caldicot)*. We have five nursing aides. All are part-time but fully trained by ourselves. Two of them narrowly missed acquiring additional diplomas in first aid and Miss Pilton, who comes in on the first Monday of the month, has just completed a local technical college course in Turkish traditional dancing, with distinction I might add. She has talked to me about providing belly dancing classes for the guests. We pride ourselves on running a home that has all the advantages of a hotel and a fully equipped modern hospital. Employing trained staff is a vital way of implementing that policy.

MR LIVINGSTONE *(He turns on the television. It is black and white and produces a mass of lines and nothing else.)* The telly is still on the blink.

MR MULLER-HAWKSMOOR: It appears that the set in this suite does have some minor fault at the present time but there is, of course, additional, supplementary audio visual equipment in the Duke of Devonshire Leisure and Recreational Area, and I am assured by our visiting consultant engineer that they will have that equipment working satisfactorily in a very short space of time. We spare no expense to ensure that our guests are happy.

MR LIVINGSTONE: That one's been on the blink for a month – ever since it caught fire and Mr Hewitt had to throw two buckets of water over it.

MR MULLER-HAWKSMOOR: Please don't exaggerate, Mr Stanley. It was a very small fire and could easily have been extinguished with the first bucket of water. The second bucket was quite unnecessary and I have issued a memo to staff and guests about the dangers of putting out electrical fires with water.

MR LIVINGSTONE: The second bucket was for the chair Miss Nightingale was sitting in. The plastic had started to melt and her jumper was smouldering. She doesn't feel the heat like she used to.

MR MULLER-HAWKSMOOR: Mr, er, Stanley, does rather like to exaggerate. I believe Mr Stanley was an estate agent before he came to us. Ha ha ha.

MR LIVINGSTONE: I was in the RAF you pompous, young buffoon. Ex bomber command. And the name is Livingstone.

MR DEREK CALDICOT *(to Mrs Caldicot)*: I'm sure you're going to be very happy here mother.

MRS CALDICOT: What's happened to my house? Did you say something had happened to it?

MR DEREK CALDICOT: Don't you worry about that. I'll deal with all those financial things for you. Selling a house is very stressful. I couldn't have you dealing with solicitors and estate agents and that sort of thing – especially when your memory starts to go a little and you begin to get confused.

MRS CALDICOT: I don't get confused. Or at least I didn't until I took those pills. And my memory is fine most of the time.

MR MULLER-HAWKSMOOR: But the pills our doctor will prescribe for you will probably make you a little forgetful. It's what I think the doctors call the side effects.

MRS CALDICOT: Why do I need to take pills?

MR DEREK CALDICOT: Of course you'll need pills, mother! All old people need to take pills whether they're necessary or not. The pills will help keep you calm and stop you wandering off.

MRS CALDICOT: But I am calm. I'm as calm as I want to be and probably calmer than I should be and come to think of it I do definitely feel a bit funny in my head since I took those pills you got for me. And I'm not going to wander off. And I like my house. Why can't I stay there?

MR DEREK CALDICOT: (laughing dismissively). Oh, you can't stay there by yourself, mother. It wouldn't be safe. I wouldn't be happy about that. What if there's a fire? Burglars? A flood? A hurricane? The roof might blow off in a storm and what would happen then?

MRS CALDICOT: I'd probably get wet and my unmentionables would be blown all around the neighbourhood.

MR MULLER-HAWKSMOOR: No, no, we wouldn't want you living alone and by yourself in a house. You need people around you: friends to provide companionship and professional, trained health workers to provide support and care when you need it and to make sure you don't forget to take your necessary medication.

MR DEREK CALDICOT: And the lovely people here will help make sure you don't forget your pills. It's very important not to miss any of your pills. And, remember, you have to take some pills to help counteract the side effects that Mr Muller-Hawksmoor mentioned.

MRS CALDICOT: What side effects?

MR DEREK CALDICOT: The side effects of the other pills you're taking!

MRS CALDICOT: But if I'm not taking pills there won't be any side effects will there?'

MR MULLER-HAWKSMOOR: (*Laughing*) Oh, you have to take pills Mrs Caldicot. All our guests take pills. Everyone takes pills. Good heavens, even I myself have been known to take a pill occasionally.

MRS CALDICOT: But what about all my things that were in the house? My furniture and so on.

MR DEREK CALDICOT: We'll deal with all that. We've arranged for a firm of house clearance specialists to move in and empty the place. And then before it goes on sale we can get some painters in to liven the place up so that we get the best possible price.

MRS CALDICOT: But I had lovely furniture. Your father and I bought it when we first got married. It was G plan and very fashionable at the time.

MR DEREK CALDICOT: Exactly, mother. It was all very old. But not old enough to be valuable. It wasn't exactly Chippendale was it?

MRS CALDICOT: And my treasures – whatever has happened to my treasures? I had a lovely porcelain giraffe that I bought in Bournemouth. And there was a fluffy dog that I won in a raffle when I was 20. And a little model of a lighthouse filled with different coloured sands. You bought me that when we had a holiday on the Isle of Wight and I always kept it on my dressing table. You were twelve at the time and you bought it with some of your holiday spending money. I've always treasured it. And what about the

Christmas decorations? We had lovely Christmas decorations that we'd collected over the years. And an artificial tree which we bought from Woolworths. It cost £7, I remember. That was a lot of money then. It was in the loft but your father used to get it down on December 20th every year and we'd decorate it and keep it up until twelfth night. And a handbag which I inherited from my mother. It was real leather and had a lot of wear left in it. All those things were part of my life and they are part of who I am. If I have to move here why can't I have my things with me? They're full of memories.

MR MULLER-HAWKSMOOR: Oh, I'm afraid we can't have the place cluttered up with old bric a brac. Fire regulations, you know. Just think how crowded the place would be if everyone brought along all their old bits and pieces. You'll have a drawer in your room where you can keep some clothes. You need to look forward, Mrs er, um, Mrs er, not backwards. Not backwards.

MRS CALDICOT: And what about all my books?

MR DEREK CALDICOT: (*Dismissively.*) Don't worry about books. The people who are taking away the furniture will deal with those.

MRS CALDICOT: But I loved those books!

MR MULLER-HAWKSMOOR: But you'd already read them! No one reads the same book twice, do they? (*He laughs sneeringly.*) It would be as daft as watching the same film more than once, or going on holiday to the same place time and time again. To be honest I don't much hold with books – the television is much better than books, you never have to worry about losing your place or spilling coffee on it or forgetting where you've put it. The television set is always where it's supposed to be. Besides, most of our guests say that they find it difficult to concentrate on a book.

MRS CALDICOT: I'm not surprised they can't concentrate if they're kept drugged.

MR DEREK CALDICOT: You don't want your life being cluttered with all those old things, mother. Onwards and upwards is what father always used to say.

MRS CALDICOT: He used to say some very silly things but I never heard him say that.

MR MULLER-HAWKSMOOR *(sniffing the air and rubbing his hands)* Is it time for lunch? I rather think it is. I can definitely smell cabbage in the air. Full of vitamins and roughage is cabbage.

Marvellous stuff. I always say that if there's one thing our guests don't go short of it's cabbage! Lots of cabbage and plenty of pills. That's the secret of a happy life.

Act II Scene 2

(The Nursing Home. This scene is set in the bedroom part of the set. Mrs Caldicot, Mr Livingstone, Mrs Peterborough and Miss Nightingale are sitting on their beds. All are in night clothes.)

MRS CALDICOT: Do they ever serve anything that doesn't have cabbage with it? Cabbage and liver, cabbage and mince and cabbage and liver again. We had a sliver of treacle tart yesterday and I found myself hunting through the custard and looking for the cabbage.

MR LIVINGSTONE: I think they did do something without cabbage about nine months ago. The cook was away with food poisoning so we had baked beans on toast for lunch and dinner until she came back. No cabbage for a whole week. It was wonderful. The cabbage industry was in despair. Cabbage farmers complained to Parliament.

MRS CALDICOT: So did the smell of cabbage disappear?

MR LIVINGSTONE: Not entirely. But it was rather overpowered by the consequences of all those baked beans.

MRS CALDICOT: (*Laughing*) I can imagine! Do you know, I haven't taken my tablets for three days now. I feel much better than I have for ages. A month in this place is as much as I can stand.

MR LIVINGSTONE: Damned good idea of yours. Put 'em under your tongue and spit 'em out when the nurse has gone.

MRS CALDICOT: Is she really a nurse?

MR LIVINGSTONE: No, not in the sense of having qualifications. But I think she had an aunt who worked as a receptionist for a local dentist. So she has some connection with the healing professions.

MRS CALDICOT: I asked her what the pills were for and she didn't seem to have the foggiest idea. She just kept saying they were to make me feel better.

MISS NIGHTINGALE: I spat my capsules and tablets out into the sink. *(She beams.)*

MRS PETERBOROUGH: I did the same. Without getting up off my bed. I'm getting to be a very good shot with a tablet but I'm not quite as accurate with a capsule. They sometimes fire off at a funny angle. And sometimes they just sort of dribble off onto the floor.

MRS CALDICOT: I think Mr Muller-Hawksmoor is getting suspicious. Yesterday, he twice asked me why we weren't all asleep.

MR LIVINGSTONE: They like to keep us well drugged. We're less trouble that way. I think most of these places are much the same. They dope all their residents with loads of pills to keep them quiet. The so-called nurses just sit in their room and watch television all day long. Once an hour, during an ad break, one of them pops out to make sure we haven't set fire to the place or tottered off into town to paint everything red and to have some fun.

MRS CALDICOT: Who prescribes all this stuff? Does a doctor ever come round?

MR LIVINGSTONE: I don't think there's been a doctor in here since 1953. I certainly haven't seen one since I've been here. And these days they let the nurses prescribe this stuff. I'm surprised they haven't thought of putting drugs into our food.

MRS CALDICOT: It's all rather depressing isn't it? We don't get many laughs in here.

MISS NIGHTINGALE: I'd like a bit of fun occasionally. Now that I am awake more often I realise that I don't much like it here. It's like being in prison.

MRS PETERBOROUGH: Just like being in prison. But worse. We never get any porridge and no one ever escapes.

MRS CALDICOT: I managed to sneak a look at the little leaflet that came with one of the pink pills we're all taking. It says they should only be taken for up to two weeks. There's a list of nasty side effects as long as your arm.

MR LIVINGSTONE: I've been taking them for over a year.

MISS NIGHTINGALE: Why do they assume that because we're old we don't want to enjoy what's rest of our lives?

MRS PETERBOROUGH: I wish they'd let us out occasionally. I feel like a prisoner. Perhaps they brought us here because we did something naughty without realising it.

MR LIVINGSTONE: Maybe we could organise an escape committee. We could make an escape rope with a few knotted sheets. We could climb down the rope and run away. *(He pauses)*. Or we could make a glider and make our escape by air. They did that in the war. We just need some wood. (*He pauses and thinks.*) Quite a lot of wood I would imagine.

MRS PETERBOROUGH: There might be a bit of a problem with the knotted sheets idea.

MR LIVINGSTONE: What's that?

MRS PETERBOROUGH: Our room is on the ground floor.

MR LIVINGSTONE: Damn! I hadn't thought of that. Bit of a snag. Well spotted Mrs Peterborough. You're going to be an invaluable member of the escape committee. And if we're on the ground floor there's a chance that the glider wouldn't have room to take off. Maybe we could tunnel our way out. We need spoons to do the digging and a scheme to get rid of the soil. You put the soil down your trousers and then sprinkle it around as you walk around. (*He walks about, showing how it's done. Miss Nightingale and Mrs Peterborough follow him.*)

MRS CALDICOT: I'm just going to walk out of here. There's no need to dig a tunnel or make a glider. (*They all look at her.*)

MISS NIGHTINGALE: What do you mean – walk out?

MRS CALDICOT: I'm just going to go! They don't lock the front door during the day time. I'll pick a quiet moment and just leave.

MISS NIGHTINGALE: You can't go! We'd miss you.

MRS PETERBOROUGH: No, you can't go!

MRS CALDICOT: I really have to go. I can't stay here a day longer.

MISS NIGHTINGALE: I'm coming with you.

MRS PETERBOROUGH: Me too!

MRS CALDICOT: No, really, you can't. I don't know where I'm going.

MR LIVINGSTONE: The men escaping from Colditz didn't worry about where they were going. They just decided to escape. We'll find somewhere to be and we'll know where we've gone when we get there. That was good enough for them and it's good enough for me.

MRS PETERBOROUGH: But we don't have our clothes! Our clothes are always locked in the dressing table or the wardrobe so that we have to stay in our nightwear.

MR LIVINGSTONE: Clever move that on the part of the camp commandant. Lock our clothes away so that we can't go anywhere.

MRS CALDICOT: But you can't come with me. I really don't know where I'm going.

MISS NIGHTINGALE: We can't stay here if you go.

MR LIVINGSTONE: All for one and one for all. We must stick together.

MRS PETERBOROUGH: Like glue.

MR LIVINGSTONE: Like friends. Best of friends.

MRS CALDICOT: (*Hugs each of the others and thinks for a moment.*)The staff hang their coats in the hall. We could borrow their coats and put them on top of what we're wearing.

MISS NIGHTINGALE: Where shall we go?

MRS CALDICOT: (*After some thought.*) We'll find a hotel, rent some rooms and have some decent food.

MR LIVINGSTONE: I'm not going anywhere where they serve cabbage.

MRS CALDICOT: Definitely not. And no more pills.

MRS PETERBOROUGH: Would we get into trouble?

MISS NIGHTINGALE: Might we get arrested?

MRS CALDICOT: No, no! What's the worst that could happen?

MR LIVINGSTONE: They could catch us and make us come back.

MRS CALDICOT: But we're already here so we wouldn't be any worse off, would we? I'm fed up with being treated like a piece of furniture. No one ever asks us what we think or what we would like to eat or if we want to take the damned pills they keep trying to push down our throats. We're just expected to keep quiet and do what we're told.

MR LIVINGSTONE: Well said, old girl! I'm game if you are!

MRS CALDICOT: If we're not coming back we'd better take all our things with us.

MR LIVINGSTONE: I haven't got anything – except my pills and I don't want those.

MISS NIGHTINGALE: (*Sadly*) They don't let us have private things here.

MRS CALDICOT: (*Looks round*) Come to think of it I haven't got anything here, either. My son Derek sold everything for me. I think he thought he was doing me a favour. All I've got left is a spare nightie and that's in the wash. I wonder what happened to the money Derek got for selling my house and my furniture. He never said anything about it. I wish I'd been allowed to keep some of my ornaments. I had a lovely little, china cat from Padstow. *(Smiles, remembering.)* It was really lovely. It had a nice smile. I wonder what happened to it. *(Sighs)*. Oh well, never mind.

MISS NIGHTINGALE *(standing up and fetching her toothbrush)*: I'm ready! *(The others collect their toothbrushes)*.

MRS CALDICOT: Have we got everything? *(They all hold up their toothbrushes. Mrs Caldicot opens the door and looks out.)* It's all clear. Let's make a break for it! *(They hurry out.)*

Act III Scene 1:

(The Hotel. A manager stands behind the bar/reception desk. The only other person there is a young woman who has a reporter's notebook and is editing some notes. She also has a tape recorder to which she listens occasionally. Mrs Caldicot et al arrive. Mrs Peterborough and Miss Nightingale look around them.)

MISS NIGHTINGALE: It's very smart here isn't it? It's big and quiet like a church.

MRS PETERBOROUGH: More like a cathedral I would say.

MR LIVINGSTONE: Don't worry about it. Our money is as good as anyone else's.

MRS CALDICOT *(suddenly realising, speaking softly)*: We haven't got any money!

MR LIVINGSTONE *(dismissively)*: A minor problem.

MRS CALDICOT: You're right. We'll worry about that later. I could put the rooms on my son's account. He's always bringing clients here.

MR LIVINGSTONE *(to the others)*: Shall I order some drinks?

MISS NIGHTINGALE: I'd like something with a cherry in it.

MR LIVINGSTONE: Anything in particular?

MISS NIGHTINGALE: No. As long as it's got a cherry in it.

MRS PETERBOROUGH: I'd like a nice cup of tea. *(Looks around)*. This is very different to the nursing home isn't it. I'm so glad we ran away.

MR LIVINGSTONE: Do you want a cherry in that?

MRS PETERBOROUGH *(thinks)*: In my cup of tea? No I don't think so. I'll have the cherry on the side. But I would like a biscuit to dunk in it. *(She looks around again.)* I'm so glad we ran away.

MRS CALDICOT: What would you like, Mr Livingstone?

MR LIVINGSTONE: I'll have a beer to celebrate our escape from the tyranny of Mr Muller-Hawksmoor and the Twilight Years Rest Home. *(The young woman with the notebook/tape recorder is now listening to the conversation.)*

MRS CALDICOT *(she goes to the reception desk/bar)*: I'd like to order some drinks please. With biscuits. *(The young woman moves from her table to one nearer to the table where Mrs Caldicot et al are sitting.)*

HOTEL MANAGER: Are you staying in the hotel, madam?

MRS CALDICOT: Oh yes, I think so. We'll need four rooms, please.

HOTEL MANAGER: And how will you be paying?

MRS CALDICOT: Oh, just put it on my son's account please. His name's Caldicot. Derek Caldicot.

HOTEL MANAGER *(who clearly knows the name)*: Certainly, Mrs Caldicot.

MRS CALDICOT: And could we have some drinks and some biscuits, please? One beer, a pot of tea for two and something with a cherry in it. Oh and some nice glacé cherries on the side.

HOTEL MANAGER: What sort of drink with the cherry in it, madam?

MRS CALDICOT: Oh I don't think it matters. As long as there's a cherry in it.

HOTEL MANAGER *(picking four keys from the rack behind him and handing them over)*: Your keys, madam. I'll bring the drinks over to your table in a moment.

MRS CALDICOT. You won't forget the biscuits, will you?

HOTEL MANAGER: No, madam.

MRS CALDICOT: Not too many boring ones. Lots of the ones with chocolate and cream fillings. And just a few plain ones for dunking.

HOTEL MANAGER: For dunking?

MRS CALDICOT: Certainly, for dunking. The Royal family dunk all the time.

HOTEL MANAGER: Of course, madam. Biscuits for dunking.

MRS CALDICOT *(going back to where the others are sitting)*. I've ordered drinks and biscuits and booked four rooms. *(She puts four keys on the table. The young woman now moves across to their table.)*

MS JACORANDA PETTIGREW *(carrying her notebook, tape recorder and drink)*: Do you mind if I join you? I'm a reporter and I couldn't help overhearing what you were saying.

MR LIVINGSTONE *(pulls over a fifth chair)*: Sit yourself down. Do you want a drink?

MS JACORANDA PETTIGREW *(sitting)*: I've got one, thanks. Did I hear you say that you'd all just escaped from somewhere?

MR LIVINGSTONE: Definitely. We broke out. Against the odds we escaped from our evil captors without a shot being fired.

MS JACORANDA PETTIGREW *(rather startled)*: Really? Where have you escaped from?

MRS CALDICOT: We were residents at the Twilight Years Rest Home.

MR LIVINGSTONE: Inmates.

MS JACORANDA PETTIGREW: Why did you have to escape?

MR LIVINGSTONE: We were drugged. We had our clothes taken from us and we were tortured with vast quantities of overcooked cabbage. Mrs Caldicot here is the leader of our escape committee.

MS JACORANDA PETTIGREW *(scribbling in her notebook)*: Is that why you're in your nighties?

MR LIVINGSTONE *(displaying a pyjama covered leg)*: And pyjamas.

MS JACORANDA PETTIGREW: *(scribbling again)* Sorry! Nightwear. I did wonder at first if you might not all be ethnic people or members of some odd religious sect.

MRS PETERBOROUGH: They took our clothes away from us.

MR LIVINGSTONE: Standard procedure in prisoner of war camps. Take away the prisoners' clothes to humiliate them; deprive them of their identity and hinder escape. *(The manager brings over a tray with the drinks and biscuits.)*

MS JACORANDA PETTIGREW *(still scribbling)*: But you did get away!

MISS NIGHTINGALE: We were going to climb down knotted sheets.

MS JACORANDA PETTIGREW: Really?

MISS NIGHTINGALE: But we didn't have to because our room was on the ground floor.

MR LIVINGSTONE: In the end, our escape was all down to brilliant planning and strong leadership.

MRS CALDICOT: We just crept out of the front door when no one was looking.

MRS PETERBOROUGH: We borrowed coats from the hooks in the hall.

MR LIVINGSTONE: I'm wearing a rather snazzy item normally worn by our camp commandant. *(Miss Nightingale stands and does a twirl to show off her anorak and nightie).*

MS JACORANDA PETTIGREW: Do you mind if I telephone my editors? I freelance for the evening paper and I also do some research for the Mike Trickle television chat show. I think they could both be interested in your story!

MR LIVINGSTONE *(hand uplifted in triumph)*: Tell the story! Let not the truth be suppressed. Expose the evil imprisonment and abuse of innocent pensioners. *(Mrs Caldicot looks rather worried. The reporter takes out a telephone and retreats to another part of the hotel lobby.)*

MRS CALDICOT: I hope we're not all going to get into trouble.

MRS PETERBOROUGH. Why should we get into trouble? We just ran away.

MISS NIGHTINGALE: They were keeping us prisoners and making us watch black and white television with lines across it.

MR LIVINGSTONE *(indignantly)*: And they were drugging us!

MRS CALDICOT: That's perfectly true. If we hadn't stopped swallowing our pills we'd all still be asleep in our beds.

MR LIVINGSTONE: Bunk beds. And it was all down to you that we stopped our drugs. Here's to Mrs Caldicot! *(They all drink to Mrs Caldicot who responds. The three women dunk biscuits in their drinks.)*

MRS PETERBOROUGH *(to Miss Nightingale)*: Aren't you going to eat your cherry?

MISS NIGHTINGALE: No. I don't like cherries. But I think these ones are very pretty. I like to look at them. *(Jacoranda returns)*

MS JACORANDA PETTIGREW: I've spoken to my newspaper editor. He wants me to do a story about your escape. And I've also spoken to a producer on the Mike Trickle show. Their star guest has just dropped out and they are absolutely desperate to have you on this evening. Will you help them out? They'll pay you a fee and cover all your expenses.

MRS CALDICOT: Me? On television? Oh, I couldn't. I wouldn't know what to say. I haven't had my hair done and I haven't got anything to wear.

MS JACORANDA PETTIGREW: The studio will do your hair and find you something wonderful to wear.

MR LIVINGSTONE: You must do it! You'll be famous. A blow for pensioner power!

MISS NIGHTINGALE: Can I have your autograph when you've been on the television?

MRS PETERBOROUGH: Will you be in colour or black and white?

MISS NIGHTINGALE: And will you have lots of lines running across you?

MRS CALDICOT *(worried)*: Oh dear. I'm really not sure about this. Whatever would Mr Caldicot say?

MRS PETERBOROUGH *(picking up the plate of biscuits)*: Have a couple of biscuits. Take that one with the jam in the middle. It'll give you energy.

MRS CALDICOT: I think I need more than a biscuit with a jam in the middle if I'm going to be on television.

MR LIVINGSTONE *(standing up)*: I'll get you a large brandy. That'll put hairs on your chest.

MRS CALDICOT *(alarmed, looks at him.)*: I do hope not!

Act IV, Scene 1

(The Television Studio. The studio consists of two empty chairs on a platform. There are one or two television cameras, operated by one or two camera persons. Mr Livingstone, Mrs Peterborough, Miss Nightingale and Jacoranda Pettigrew are all sitting in the 'real' audience.)

MIKE TRICKLE *(wearing a bad wig and bouncing out onto the stage with arms aloft in greeting)*: Hullo, hullo, hullo. Good evening and an enormously sincere welcome from the very, very bottom of a very, very large heart. *(A man walks across the stage carrying a board which says CLAP.)* Thank you, thank you. I love you all so very, very much. Thank you to those of you at home who have tuned in and a wonderful thank you to our studio audience who have braved the elements, public transport, car park vultures and other horrors to be here with us tonight. *(He beams for a moment.)* We have a very special guest for you on today's Mike Trickle show. You won't have heard of Thelma Caldicot, she's not a big star yet, but when I heard about her I knew we had to have her on the show tonight. I always insist on being the first with the great interviews, first with the scoops, so that you have the very best of entertainment and the very best of current affairs. So I dumped the star guest we had planned, and told him to stay home and watch the show instead of being on it, and I personally made sure that we booked Mrs Caldicot for you. *(The man with the board which says CLAP walks across the stage again.)* I have to tell you that you, the audience, are the only people who really matter in my life – and three ex-wives still on the payroll will confirm that. (Laughs). So, now, without any more ado, let me introduce this evening's very special, surprise, star guest –Mrs Thelma Caldicot. Let's have a big hand for her. *(Mike does some clapping. Thelma walks onto the stage looking very nervous. She is wearing a very posh dress and has had her hair done. She looks a star.)* Come on, Mrs Caldicot, come over here and sit down and talk to me, the audience and our millions of viewers at home. *(Thelma looks around at the cameras and the audience. Mr*

Livingstone and the others stand up and clap enthusiastically. Mike and Mrs Caldicot both sit.) So, Thelma, may I call you Thelma *(he doesn't wait for an answer)*, welcome to the Mike Trickle show!

MRS CALDICOT *(nervously and barely audibly)*: Thank you.

MIKE TRICKLE: No need to be nervous. I know you're not really a nervous person, Thelma. You're going to be the big news story in tomorrow's papers because you led a walk out of residents at the Twilight Years Rest Home. It is, so I am told, the first ever walk out of residents from an old folks' home. When did you become a revolutionary, Thelma? Would you describe yourself as a revolutionary or as an anarchist, by the way?

MRS CALDICOT *(clearly startled)*: Oh, I wouldn't...I don't think...I don't know...

MIKE TRICKLE: You don't know! You wouldn't? *(He turns to the audience and pulls a face)*. Really, that's not good enough, Thelma. You have a responsibility, not to me, I don't matter, but to your colleagues and to the public at large. You led a walk out. You've started a new movement. You say you walked out because you don't like cabbage but don't you think that was selfish and irresponsible? Wasn't it really a rather over-dramatic response to a childish dislike of cabbage – a dislike, incidentally, which the National Cabbage Board tells me is quite unfounded. Cabbage, so say the experts, is an excellent form of vital nutrients – especially for older citizens. I don't like beetroot but I'm not going to walk out of the studio in protest! *(The man walks across with the CLAP board.)*

MRS CALDICOT: That's not what happened. I thought the smell of cabbage was pretty nasty and they served up cabbage with everything but that's only a tiny part of the story.

MIKE TRICKLE: But wasn't it a tiny reason for a big deed? If everyone had a paddy and a sulk and insisted that they went on television to tell the world about it, all just because they didn't like their vegetables the world would be a pretty turbulent place wouldn't it? *(The man hurries across the stage holding the CLAP board.)*

MRS CALDICOT: Why are you being so aggressive? I didn't want to attract attention to myself at all but the nice lady I met at the hotel this afternoon said your star guest had cancelled and she asked me to help you out. I only said I'd come on the programme because she said you were desperate. *(Mrs Caldicot's friends stand up and applaud.)*

MIKE TRICKLE: But these are elderly people. *(He lowers and softens his voice.)* They are old people who are vulnerable and easily influenced. They need their medication and their regular meals.

MRS CALDICOT: Now you're just being patronising. Why does everyone think they can patronise older people all the time? You're like those people in shops and offices and on the telephone who talk down to pensioners and treat them as though they're members of some sub-species, or aliens from another planet. If I have to ring the gas people they always want to know my date of birth. I can't imagine why but they do. Maybe you're not allowed to have gas if you're too old. And then when I've told them they always say 'well done' as if I've just discovered a new way to split the atom or won a gold medal in the Olympics. All I've done is get my date of birth right but they congratulate me as if I've really astonished them with my brilliance. Why do people under 40 always assume that anyone over 60 must be senile, and then act all surprised and delighted when you turn out not to be? And why am I invisible in shops? I stood at the counter in the Post Office one day and a girl of about 18 came up, completely ignored me, and asked for a book of stamps. She and the fellow behind the counter behaved as though I were completely invisible. They just chatted away as if I weren't there at all. When the girl had finished and had tottered off, I asked the man behind the glass if I could have my turn. I said 'I'm sorry I'm not 18 and wearing a tight top but am I still allowed to buy stamps?' He looked at me as if I were barking mad, closed his partition and buggered off so I obviously really was invisible. And you're the same. I'm surprised you can even see me sitting here.

MR LIVINGSTONE *(standing up and calling out)*: We may be old but that doesn't mean we like being pushed around and treated like idiots.

MRS CALDICOT *(looks at Mr Livingstone and waves to him. She's getting more confident now)*: Just because people are old it doesn't mean that they can't make up their own minds about things. Just because people are in their 70s, 80s and 90s it doesn't mean that they have to put up with being drugged and bullied.

MIKE TRICKLE: But even if you decided to walk out of the nursing home because you didn't like the cabbage, that wasn't any reason to drag your fellow residents with you! Do you think it was responsible to drag them out of their warm, comfortable home, where they were receiving careful, professional attention and make them follow you into the cold and frightening wilderness? Aren't you the bully?

MRS CALDICOT: I didn't make anyone do anything!

MR LIVINGSTONE *(and the other two)*: No, she didn't!

MIKE TRICKLE: Are you now claiming that you are so charismatic that these people just followed you? *(He turns to the audience and pulls a face.)* You don't look that charismatic to me.

MRS CALDICOT: No! I'm not claiming to be charismatic or a leader or anything like that. I'm just trying to tell you what happened.

MIKE TRICKLE: Don't you think you were taking a big risk – walking out as you did?

MRS CALDICOT: What's the point of life if you don't take chances occasionally – and stick up for yourself and the people around you?

MIKE TRICKLE: Aren't you a bit old to be taking chances? *(He pulls another face at the audience.)*

MRS CALDICOT: There you go again – being ageist. I don't think I took enough chances in my life.

MIKE TRICKLE: Really?

MRS CALDICOT: No! What had I got to lose? I was fed up with being treated as a non-person. A lot of old people who are my age and older don't have the option of walking out. They're stuck where they are. They have to put up with being bullied and drugged and treated like naughty children. Yes, I did what I did for me and my new friends but I also did it for the people who are too frail to stand up for themselves.

MIKE TRICKLE: But you're an old woman. You should be sitting at home watching television not up here battling away on some curious cabbage crusade!

MRS CALDICOT: Why are you being so rude and aggressive? Why do you keep making faces to the audience when the camera isn't on you? How would you like it if I asked you why you wore such a silly wig? And does your wife know about that blonde girl who came out of your dressing room? She only looked about 20, and the nice lady who did my hair said she lives at home with her mum and works in the make-up department. *(Mr Livingstone et al cheer and laugh.)*

MIKE TRICKLE *(disbelievingly)*: What did you say?

MRS CALDICOT: I asked how you'd like it if I asked you why you wore such a silly wig. And if your wife…

MIKE TRICKLE *(standing up and talking over Mrs Caldicot)*: Thank you, Mrs Caldicot. That's all for this week's show. Next week we'll have another wonderful guest for you. *(He waves to the audience and leaves the stage. He is immediately followed by the two cameramen. The main lights go off. Mike is offstage but we hear him shouting.)* Who let that woman on my show? This is a disaster. How did she find out about the wig? No one is supposed to know about the wig. And someone had better get my wife on the phone… *(Mrs Caldicot is now standing on the stage, ignored and alone. Her chums, who were sitting in the audience, climb onto the stage and talk to her. Derek, who was also in the audience, climbs onto the stage.)*

MR DEREK CALDICOT: That was the most disgraceful display I have ever seen. I have never been so embarrassed in my life. I don't know what my wife will say. She's a huge fan of Mike Trickle. She's got his pop-up book of celebrity chitchat and has all his cookery books. You humiliated the poor man. How could you do that, mother? Don't you realise the trouble you've caused? I've just had my boss on the phone. He went ballistic. He told me the other residents are leaving the Twilight Years Rest Home in droves. Some are being fetched by worried relatives. Some have just walked out and gone to stay with friends. You've started a revolution, mother! My boss is so angry that he's planning to close the place. He's talking of putting it up for sale as a damage limitation exercise. He's terrified the fuss will spread to the rest of the chain. We have 73 nursing homes throughout the country for heaven's sake!

JENKINS *(who has wandered on, also from the audience)*: May I offer my congratulations on a very spirited performance? *(He holds out a hand)*. That was the best piece of live television I've seen for a long time. I'm sorry – I should have introduced myself. My name is Jenkins. I'm the editor of The Sunday Globe. I found your story fascinating and I'd like to interview you for the paper.

MRS CALDICOT: Oh, I'm not sure that I want any more publicity, thank you very much.

JENKINS: I promise you it will be a very sympathetic piece. And you have an important story that needs to be told. People shouldn't be treated without respect just because of their age. We have laws which stop discrimination and prejudice because of sex or race so why should we allow discrimination because of age? Old people need a champion – and you're that champion.

MRS CALDICOT: You really don't want to attack me – as Mike Trickle just did?

JENKINS: No, of course not. Our readers will be sympathetic and very much on your side. Why would we publish a piece guaranteed to alienate them? I can tell you now that Mike Trickle made quite a mistake this evening. A moment ago one of the producers told me that they've been inundated with calls from viewers supporting you and criticising Trickle. And it wasn't just older viewers who were angry. The producer told me that they've had a lot of calls from younger viewers who realise that one day they may be old themselves! Mr Trickle is going to find himself very unpopular tomorrow – and not just with his wife. And you're going to find yourself quite the heroine!

MRS CALDICOT: Really?

JENKINS: Oh yes! And if you agree to talk to us we'll pay you a very substantial fee.

MRS CALDICOT: You'll pay me?

JENKINS: Oh yes! And, I suspect, considerably more than Mr Trickle's show paid you. And you're going to need some money now.

MRS CALDICOT: The television people promised to pay me £100. But they also said they'd pay my hotel bill for the night.

JENKINS *(smiling)*: They're notoriously stingy when it comes to paying guests. They get a lot of actors and singers who want to be on the programme to plug their latest film or record and so they can get away with paying ridiculously small fees.

MRS CALDICOT: Mind you, they don't know yet but my bill will be for four rooms and quite a lot of room service.

JENKINS *(laughing)*: Serves them right. We'll happily pay your hotel bill for as long as you need to be there. And we'll also pay you well for your story. How does £25,000 sound?

MRS CALDICOT *(shocked)*: £25,000? Oh dear me.

JENKINS: Quite right. Nowhere near enough. My apologies. Does £50,000 sound better?

MRS CALDICOT *(more shocked)*: It sounds rather pleasant. And you won't be horrid about me? You promise?

JENKINS: I promise. We certainly won't be horrid about you. You will be our heroine. A spokeswoman for your generation. *(He holds out his hand. Mrs Caldicot takes it and they shake on the deal.)*

Act V Scene 1:

(The Lobby at the Twilight Years Rest Home. Mrs Caldicot, her pals and a greasy young man in a cheap suit enter the Twilight Years Rest home. The whole place now looks very scruffy and broken down. The young man, who carries a pile of brochures, is an estate agent.)

ESTATE AGENT: I understand that you're looking for a large house for yourself and some friends?

MRS CALDICOT: That's right!

ESTATE AGENT: Until a week ago this was a nursing home run by a large property company. They had some trouble and closed the place down very quickly – I think they must have decided to cut their losses.

MRS CALDICOT: It needs some work doing.

ESTATE AGENT: Just small stuff. Nothing a decent handyman couldn't deal with. Lick of paint here and there.

MRS CALDICOT *(looking around)*: Hmm. No, I suppose we could do something with it.

ESTATE AGENT: We have contact details for a fellow who is apparently willing to take a job here as general handyman and gardener. He knows the place quite well, I understand. Lost his position when the place closed and now he's rather desperate for a job.

MRS CALDICOT: That sounds helpful.

ESTATE AGENT: Would you like me to give him a ring?

MRS CALDICOT: That would be marvellous! *(The estate agent pulls out a mobile phone and makes a call. Mrs Caldicot and the others look around. The agent talks quietly for a moment or two and then closes his phone and puts it back in his pocket.)*

ESTATE AGENT: That's all settled. He'll be here in a couple of minutes.

MRS CALDICOT: It certainly looks as if the previous owners left in a hurry.

ESTATE AGENT: Yes, I believe they did. And now they're keen for a quick sale. They want to get rid of the place. Bad memories for them, I think.

MRS CALDICOT: I wonder why!

ESTATE AGENT: Can't imagine. Some sort of bad publicity I think. I heard it was something to do with a former resident.

MRS CALDICOT: So the place is going cheap?

ESTATE AGENT: It's very reasonably priced. Confidentially, I think they'll entertain quite a low offer for a quick sale. Do you have money for the deposit?

MRS CALDICOT: Oh yes, I've got £50,000 for the deposit.

ESTATE AGENT: Oh that would be marvellous. We could easily fix you up with a loan for the rest. Would you like me to show you round?

MRS CALDICOT: No, I don't think that will be necessary.

ESTATE AGENT: I tell you what – I'll pop back to the office and get a contract sorted out. You look around by yourselves and this chap should be here shortly. When you've talked to him, come along to the office and we'll get the deal done and dusted. *(He leaves. Moments later the bell goes. Mrs Caldicot opens the door. Mr Muller-Hawksmoor is standing there.)*

MR MULLER-HAWKSMOOR *(startled)*: Oh, Mrs Caldicot! *(Pause)*. The agent told me they had a buyer who, er, might want a handyman.

MRS CALDICOT: The buyer would be me. And yes we do need a handyman. Actually, a handyman-cum-gardner.

MR MULLER-HAWKSMOOR: Oh yes, gardening too. I could do that.

MRS CALDICOT: We just need someone to do all the odd jobs.

MR LIVINGSTONE: Cleaning out the drains.

MISS NIGHTINGALE: Emptying the bedpans.

MRS PETERBOROUGH: I expect there will be a lot of drain cleaning to be done. And bedpans.

MR MULLER-HAWKSMOOR: Oh, yes. I could do drains. Definitely. I think I'd be quite good at drains.

MRS CALDICOT: And lots of weeding.

MR MULLER-HAWKSMOOR: I'm very good at weeding.

MRS CALDICOT: And your first job will be to put up a big sign in the kitchen. *(She finds a piece of board and a thick pen or some chalk and writes on it quickly. When she's finished she turns the board round. She has written: 'No Cabbage Allowed'. The other three see what she has written and they cheer.)*

MR MULLER-HAWKSMOOR: Would you like me to put that up now for you?

MRS CALDICOT: Yes, straight away please. *(Mr Muller-Hawksmoor hurries off with the board. Mrs Caldicot turns to her three companions.)* Do you know, I think we can safely say that we won the Cabbage War! *(Mr Livingstone, who has been rummaging in a cupboard, produces a bottle of champagne and four glasses. He opens the bottle and pours the champagne as the curtain falls, the lights go out and/or whatever else happens to denote the end of the evening's entertainment.)*

This play may be performed by amateur dramatic societies without charge.

For permission to perform the play 'Mrs Caldicot's Cabbage War' please write to: publishing@mail.com giving details of your proposed date and venue, together with your name and email address.

Printed scripts are available on Amazon and since these are copyright Vernon Coleman should not be copied without permission. The play must not be altered without consultation with the author. Please credit Vernon Coleman as the author of 'Mrs Caldicot's Cabbage War' on all programmes, posters and promotional material whether printed or electronic. Thank you.

Other books about Mrs Caldicot, all written by Vernon Coleman, are: Mrs Caldicot's Knickerbocker Glory, Mrs Caldicot's Oyster Parade and Mrs Caldicot's Turkish Delight. There is also an Omnibus edition containing all four books. This is entitled `Mrs Caldicot Omnibus Edition'.

Author Biography

Sunday Times bestselling author Vernon Coleman qualified as a doctor in 1970 and has worked both in hospitals and as a principal in general practice. Vernon Coleman is a multi-million selling author. He has written over 100 books which have sold over three million copies in the UK, been in bestseller lists around the world and been translated into 26 languages. Several of his books have been on the bestseller lists and in the UK paperback editions of his books have been published by Pan, Penguin, Corgi, Arrow, Century, RKP, Mandarin and Star among many others. His novel 'Mrs Caldicot's Cabbage War' was turned into a successful, award winning movie. He has presented numerous programmes on television and radio, including several series based on his best-selling book Bodypower which was voted one of the 100 most popular books by British readers.

Vernon Coleman has written columns for the Daily Star, Sun, Sunday Express, Planet on Sunday and The People and has contributed over 5,000 articles, columns and reviews to 100 leading British publications including Daily Telegraph, Sunday Telegraph, Guardian, Observer, Sunday Times, Daily Mail, Mail on Sunday, Daily Express, Woman, Woman's Own, Punch and Spectator. His columns and articles have also appeared in hundreds of leading magazines and newspapers throughout the rest of the world. He edited the British Clinical Journal and founded and edited the European Medical Journal. For twenty years he wrote a column which was syndicated to over 40 leading regional newspapers in the UK and to papers all around the world.

In the UK, Vernon Coleman was the TV AM doctor on breakfast TV and the first networked television Agony Aunt, working on the BBC. Many millions consulted his Telephone Doctor advice lines, and for six years he wrote a monthly newsletter which had subscribers in 17 countries.

For over 30 years he has had a website (www.vernoncoleman.com) and the latest figures show that between 25 and 30 million people read his web articles each month.

Vernon Coleman has a medical degree, and an honorary science doctorate. He has worked for the Open University in the UK and was an honorary Professor of Holistic Medical Sciences at the Open International University based in Sri Lanka. He worked as a general practitioner for ten years (resigning from the NHS after being fined for refusing to divulge confidential information about his patients to State bureaucrats) and has organised numerous campaigns both for people and for animals. He has given evidence to both the House of Commons and the House of Lords in the UK. He can ride a bicycle and swim, though not at the same time. He likes animals, cafés and collecting cigarette cards. Vernon Coleman is a bibliophile and has a library larger than most towns. He used to enjoy cricket when it was played as a sport by gentlemen but lost heart when the authorities started painting advertisements on the grass. He loves log fires and making bonfires.

Since 1999 he has been very happily married to the professional artist and author, Donna Antoinette Coleman to whom he is devoted and with whom he has co-written five books. They live in the delightful if isolated village of Bilbury in Devon where they have designed for themselves a unique world to sustain and nourish them in these dark and difficult times. They rarely leave home.

For more information please visit: www.vernoncoleman.com or see his author page on Amazon.

Printed in Great Britain
by Amazon

44351139R00030